The ay Dulce

written &
illustrated by:

Mr. Lopez's &
Ms. Hofmann's
2nd grade classes

Copyright 2014 Red Road Books

ISBN-13: 978-1499690910
ISBN-10: 1499690916
BISAC: Juvenile Fiction / Fairy Tales & Folklore / Adaptations

EDITED AND FORMATTED BY: KELLY CARLOS
For more information about this book, please visit:

www.redroadbooks.com

A HUGE gracias to:
Ms. Hofmann & Mr. Lopez
for all their hard work
in the dual language program
at Washington Elementary.

Me antoja un dulce. ¿Y tú?

Another HUGE gracias to:
Jose Carlos & Quetzalli Carlos
for all their artistic help
with our illustrations!

Dulce! Dulce de mango is hot, hot, HOT! Some-one dipped him in *chile* and salt. And then, *¿tu crees?* they trapped him in *plástico*.

"Help! *¡Ayúdenme!*" cried Dulce.

¡Que suerte! A little girl came into the store. She begged her *papi* for $.50 because tomorrow is her birthday!

"Hmm, which one do I want?" thought Rosita. "Mmm, there's that mango one with *chile* and salt!

Rosita grabbed *dulce de mango* and ripped off the wrapper.

"Yes! *Soy libre!*" thought Dulce.

Rosita stuck out her tongue and gave it a big LICK!

"Eww! *Babas!*" screamed Dulce. "Wait a minute *chiquita*. I know I'm hot, but I don't need your tongue to cool me off. How about going to a pool?"

Rosita dropped Dulce in her surprise. Who ever heard of a talking *paleta?*

Dulce jumped to his feet and started running across the train tracks.

"Hey! *¿a dónde vas Dulce?* yelled Rosita.

Dulce stuck out his tongue and sang:

Just then, an amigo from class walked by.

"Hey, Luis! *¡Ven!* Help me catch that *dulce*. I will share it with you!" yelled Rosita.

Both kids ran fast after that candy.

But Dulce ran faster. He stayed one step ahead, singing:

"*Corre, corre,* I'm sweet and I'm hot. I'm the *dulce de mango,* and I won't be caught!"

"Hey! There's that crazy squirrel, always flying through the pine trees," yelled Luis.

"Oye, *ardilla loca*," called Rosita. "You're super *rápida*! Help us catch that *dulce* and we will share a piece."

They all ran and ran. But Dulce stayed one step ahead, singing:

"*Corre, corre*, I'm sweet and I'm hot. I'm the *dulce de mango*, and I won't be caught!"

"Hey! There's that stray cat always pooping in my yard," yelled Luis.

"Oye, *gato gordo*," called Rosita. "You're super *rápido*! Help us catch that *dulce* and we will share a piece."

They all ran and ran. But Dulce stayed one step ahead, singing:

"*Corre, corre,* I'm sweet and I'm hot. I'm the *dulce de mango,* and I won't be caught!"

"Hey! There's that rascal dog always jumping over my fence," yelled Luis.

"Oye, *perro travieso*," called Rosita. "You're super *rápido*! Help us catch that *dulce* and we will share a piece."

They all ran and ran. But Dulce stayed one step ahead, singing:

"*Corre, corre,* I'm sweet and I'm hot. I'm the *dulce de mango,* and I won't be caught!"

Dulce ran until the end of town. But, *ay, ay, ay...* there's a cliff!

"If I jump, I will break into *pedacitos!*" cried Dulce.

"Not if I help you," said an eagle from a branch up above. "Hop on my *colita*. I can fly you to safety."

"You just want to eat me like everyone else," said Dulce.

"Didn't you ever go to school?" laughed the eagle. "I am a carnivore. You are full of sugar, not *carne*. So, ¡*no gracias!*

Dulce saw all the others catching up. The birthday *niña*, the *amigo*, the *ardilla loca*, the pooping *gato*, and the *perro travieso* were just around the last pine tree.

Dulce hopped on eagle's tail and cried, "¡Vámonos! Let's fly!"
   He held onto the eagle's feathers, but felt his grip getting loose.

"*Espérate*, I think I am slipping," cried Dulce.

"Climb onto my back so you don't fall," said the eagle.

"*Espérate*, I am still slipping," cried Dulce.

"Climb onto my head so you don't fall," said the eagle.

"*Espérate*, I am still slipping," cried Dulce.

"Let me hold you in my beak, so you don't fall," said the eagle.

Now, even though dulce was just sugar, chile and salt, he was smart! He once heard a story about a silly gingerbread man who trusted a fox. Isn't the eagle a predator, just like the fox?

Just as the eagle was about to snatch him in his beak, Dulce saw something blue below. A lake! *Agua!* Relief from all this hot *chile!*

Dulce let go of the eagle's feathers and dropped to the water below. Just as he splashed into the nice cool *agua*, a *niño* swam by...

"Look what I found, *mamá!*" the boy cheered. And he stuck Dulce right into his mouth.

Chapolin colorado,
este cuento de *dulce de mango*
se ha acabado.

KC   Blanca   Alexis T.

Jazmine

Laila   Alejandro

Sherlyn   Patty

Heidi M.   Leticia
          Natalia

Alejandra

Lupe   Jaqueline

Victoria   Benito
Dalia   Xarol ♡

Gael   Fabiola
Jesus H.
           Carlos jr.
Delia.S
Oswaldo
           Adrian.R

Aliyah Osmar

Alexis B.   Johnathan   Tonalli

Jada   Roxanna

Perla   Geovana

Natalie

Abriyel   Haysin
Alonso

Josh

Roman   Kevin

Quetzal

Jose Jesus

Juan   Michael

Julio

Made in the USA
San Bernardino, CA
03 March 2016